ROOMMATES
and RACHEL

ROOMMATES and RACHEL

Kathryn O. Galbraith

illustrated by Mark Graham

it's a girl

name: Rachel
born: December 2
wt. 7 lb. 2 oz. ht. 21 in.

Margaret K. McElderry Books

NEW YORK

Collier Macmillan Canada

TORONTO

Maxwell Macmillan International Publishing Group

NEW YORK OXFORD SINGAPORE SYDNEY

Margaret K. McElderry Books
Macmillan Publishing Company
866 Third Avenue
New York, NY 10022

Collier Macmillan Canada, Inc.
1200 Eglinton Avenue East
Suite 200
Don Mills, Ontario M3C 3N1

First Edition
Printed in the United States of America
10 9 8 7 6 5 4 3 2 1

Library of Congress Cataloging-in-Publication Data
Galbraith, Kathryn Osebold.
Roommates and Rachel / Kathryn O. Galbraith ; illustrated by Mark
Graham.
p.   cm.
Summary: Beth and Mimi find their lives changed in both good and
bad ways after the arrival of their new baby sister, Rachel.
ISBN 0-689-50520-5
[1. Babies—Fiction.   2. Sisters—Fiction.]   I. Graham, Mark,
1952-   ill.   II. Title.
PZ7.G1303Rq   1991
[Fic]—dc20   90-34768   CIP   AC

To Barbara, Cathy, Nancy, and Pat.
And once again to Steve.

K. O. G.

Chapter One

Creak, creak.

Mama sat in the old rocking chair, rocking the new baby, Rachel.

Beth and her big sister, Mimi, sat on the couch. They were reading the Sunday comics.

"Girls," Mama said, "would you please bring me a diaper?"

"Babies sure need a lot of diapers," Mimi whispered. She

held her nose. "Pee-you!"

Mimi and Beth giggled.

They went into the baby's room. Before Rachel was born, it was Beth's room. Now Beth shared Mimi's room. They were roommates.

Mimi grabbed a diaper off the changing table.

Beth looked around the room. "It's not fair," she said. "Look at all of Rachel's toys. It's not even Christmas yet. Why do new babies get all the presents? What about new sisters?

"One, two, three." Beth counted three woolly lambs. On the floor was a giant panda bear from Grandpa Jack.

"It's not fair," she said again.

Mimi held up a fuzzy brown-and-white puppy. "I like this one," she said. "It looks like Willie."

Just then the doorbell rang. Willie started to bark.

"I bet it's more people to see Rachel," Mimi said.

Beth nodded. "And I know what they're going to say." She made her voice high and squeaky. "'Well, Beth, how do you like being a big sister?'"

Mimi and Beth laughed.

"Girls," Mama called. "Mrs. Fletcher is here."

Sometimes Mrs. Fletcher baby-sat for Mimi and Beth, but

today she brought Rachel a soft
yellow lamb.

"That makes four," Mimi
whispered.

"Well, Beth," Mrs. Fletcher
said, "how do you like being a
big sister?"

"Fine," answered Beth in a
high, squeaky voice.

Mimi started to giggle.

"Oh, girls, don't be so silly,"
Mama said.

Mama laid Rachel on the couch
to change her diaper. Rachel
kicked her feet and fussed.

Mrs. Fletcher said, "Look at
those tiny hands. And what dear
little toes. Isn't she darling?"

Beth didn't think Rachel was
darling at all. She thought Rachel
looked like a pink frog.

After Mrs. Fletcher left, Beth
said, "What's so great about
babies? Babies can't do anything.
Rachel can't even talk yet."

For once Mimi agreed with
her. "I know. She can't even say
'Mimi'!"

Chapter Two

The next day was Monday.

"Just think," Mimi said. "Only eleven more days till Christmas."

Eleven more days! Beth couldn't wait. "What do you want from Santa?" she asked.

"A giraffe!" Mimi said.

Beth laughed. That's what Mimi said every year.

Mama came out of Rachel's room. "Shh," she whispered. "I just put Rachel down for her nap."

Mama looked tired. She lay down on the couch. "Would you please be very quiet," she said. "I'm just going to rest for a little while."

Mimi and Beth tiptoed into the kitchen.

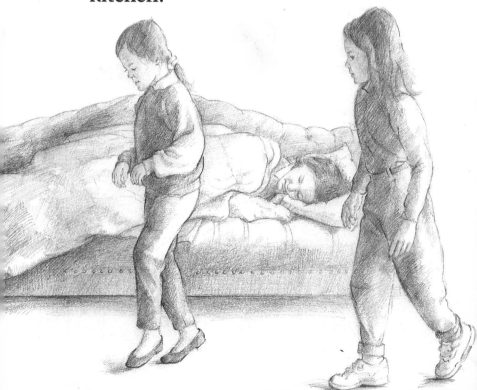

Mimi had an idea. "Let's surprise Mama. Let's make Christmas tree ornaments."

Mimi got out green paper and red paper and a bottle of glue. Beth took the scissors from the drawer.

Mimi cut out four green Christmas trees. Then she cut out eight little red balls and glued them onto her trees.

Beth couldn't decide what to make. She peeked over Mimi's shoulder. Then she made four red Christmas trees with eight green balls on them.

"Copycat!" Mimi said.

"I am not," answered Beth.

"Girls," Mama called. "Stop fighting!"

Mimi and Beth looked at each other. They weren't fighting. Not really.

Mimi said, "Now Mama is mad at us, and it's your fault."

"It is not!" Beth said.

"Girls!" Mama came into the kitchen. "I want you to stop fighting!"

Mama saw their green and red Christmas trees on the table. Then she saw the little bits of green and red paper all over the floor. "What a mess!" she said. "I want you to clean this right up."

Mimi and Beth were very quiet. They swept up every little

piece of paper. Then they went into their room.

Mimi sat on her bed.

Beth sat on her own bed.

"I don't think Mama liked the surprise," Beth said.

"It's not fair," Mimi said. She put the Christmas trees away in her drawer. "Mama never gets mad at Rachel."

Suddenly Willie began to bark.

"Willie, hush!" Mama called. But it was too late. Rachel began to cry. Willie had woken her up.

"Bad dog," Mama scolded.

"Poor Willie," said Beth. "It's not his fault."

Mimi nodded. "He always barks at the mailman."

Mimi and Beth opened the
door to their room. "Here,
Willie," they called.

Mimi gave Willie a hug. "Poor
Willie," she said. "I bet you wish
Rachel was somebody else's baby."

Willie licked her ear.

Mimi sighed. "I know just
how you feel," she whispered.

Chapter Three

It was almost Christmastime. There were just two more days of school.

"Mama, guess what?" said Mimi. "We're having a party on Friday."

"A Christmas and Hanukkah party!" added Beth. "We're having one, too."

"In my class," Mimi said, "we have to bring cookies and something special to share."

"In *my* class," Beth said, "we have to bring cookies and something special to share, too."

Mama smiled. "We can make some Christmas cookies tonight," she said.

"Can we make the Santa Claus ones?" asked Mimi.

"Can we make the Christmas tree ones?" asked Beth.

"We can make them all," Mama said. "You can both help."

After dinner, Mama got out the flour and sugar and butter. She handed the bottles of red sprinkles and green sprinkles to Mimi. She gave the bottle of silver candy balls to Beth.

Just then Rachel began to cry.

"Oh, dear," Mama said. "I'll be right back."

Mimi and Beth waited while Mama changed Rachel's diaper.

Rachel still cried.

Mama sighed. "Now I think she's hungry." She warmed up a bottle of milk. "I'll be right back," she said again.

Mimi and Beth leaned against the kitchen counter.

"Rachel spoils everything," whispered Beth.

Mimi nodded. "I bet we never make any Christmas cookies tonight," she said.

"I bet you do." Daddy came into the kitchen. "Here, I'll help

you. I'm a great cookie maker."

Daddy got out the big jar of peanut butter and the box of brown sugar.

Mimi looked at Beth. Beth looked at Mimi.

"Can you make peanut butter cookies for a Christmas and Hanukkah party?" asked Mimi.

"Sure," Daddy said. "Peanut butter cookies are good anytime."

Making cookies with Daddy
was fun. Daddy whistled while
he mixed the dough. Then Mimi
rolled the dough into little round
balls. Beth pressed the balls into
flat cookies with a fork.

Mimi and Beth looked at the
cookies. They looked like nice
peanut butter cookies, but...

"I know what," Mimi said. "Let's put the sprinkles on them!"

Mimi and Beth took turns sprinkling the cookies. Then they added a silver candy ball to the middle of each one.

Daddy put the cookies into the oven to bake. As soon as the cookies were cool, Daddy, Mimi, and Beth each tried one.

"Mmmm, good!" Daddy said.

Mimi nodded. "And they're pretty, too."

Beth took another bite. They were good and they were pretty. She just hoped Daddy was right. She hoped peanut butter cookies were good anytime—even for a Christmas and Hanukkah party.

Chapter Four

That night Mimi looked through all her drawers for something special to share on Friday.

Beth looked through all her boxes.

When Mama came in to kiss them good-night, Mimi said, "We never have anything special to share."

Mama held up Mimi's pink

shell necklace. "Why don't you take this? And, Beth, you can take your ballet slippers."

Mimi and Beth shook their heads.

"I took my slippers last time," said Beth.

"And everyone has seen my necklace a zillion times," Mimi added.

After Mama turned out the light, Mimi whispered, "I wish I had something really special to share." She thought a minute. Then she giggled. "I know what! I'll take Willie. Everybody would love that."

Beth laughed. "Maybe I'll take Rachel."

"Rachel!" Mimi sat up in bed.
"Hey, what a great idea!"

Beth sat up, too. "Oh, Mimi,
you can't take a real baby to
school."

"Why not?" said Mimi. "Everybody would be so surprised."

Mimi couldn't wait to ask
Mama. She jumped out of bed
and ran into the living room.

What would Mama say? Beth
couldn't wait to hear. She
jumped out of bed and ran into
the living room, too.

"Mama," said Mimi. "Can
you bring Rachel to my party on
Friday? Oh, please!"

"Rachel?" Mama looked
surprised. Then she smiled.
"Well, we'll see."

24

"That means yes," whispered Mimi.

"It could mean no," Beth whispered back.

The next afternoon Mama called Mimi's teacher. "We'll let Mr. Cohen decide," she said. Mimi stood by the phone and listened.

"Hey, Beth!" Mimi came running into their room. "Mr. Cohen said I can bring Rachel to my party. He said it's a wonderful idea."

Beth looked up. "He did?" She thought a minute. "Wait, maybe I want Rachel to come to my party, too."

"Copycat!" said Mimi.

"I am not," Beth said. "Besides, it was my idea."

Mama called Beth's teacher. Mrs. Wheeler thought it was a wonderful idea, too.

Mimi danced around the room. "I can't wait till tomorrow," she said.

That night, Beth couldn't go to sleep. She was thinking about the party. What if everybody thought babies were dumb? What if they all laughed?

"Psst, Mimi?"

Mimi didn't answer.

Beth sighed. She wished Rachel wasn't coming to school after all. Now she wished she was bringing her ballet slippers instead.

Chapter Five

Mimi stared at the clock over the classroom door.

Tick, tick, tick.

Soon Mama and Rachel would be here. Mimi's heart beat faster.

"Today," Mr. Cohen said, "we are going to have our party with Mrs. Wheeler's class. Mimi and her sister Beth have something very special to share with you."

Everyone looked at Mimi.

Mimi looked down at her desk. Her heart beat even faster. What if everybody thought babies were dumb? What if everybody laughed? Now Mimi wished Mama and Rachel weren't coming. Now she wished she had brought her shell necklace instead.

"Okay, class," Mr. Cohen said. "Let's line up."

Mimi stood in line with her friend Kelly. Behind her stood Danny and Timothy.

"Psst, Mimi," whispered Danny. "What did you and Beth bring?"

"Yeah," said Timothy. "What's so special?"

"No talking, please," Mr. Cohen said. "Let's show Mrs. Wheeler's class how quiet we can be."

Mimi was as quiet as a mouse. She wished she *were* a mouse.

When Mimi walked into Beth's class, there was Mama. She was sitting in Mrs. Wheeler's chair. On her lap was Rachel.

Danny poked Timothy. "Look, a baby!"

Mama smiled. "This is Mimi's and Beth's new little sister," she said. "Her name is Rachel."

Rachel was wrapped up in her yellow blanket. All they could see were her nose and her eyes.

Mama opened the yellow blanket. Then she opened the

white blanket inside. There was
Rachel in her pink winter pajamas.

"Gosh," Danny said. "She
sure is little." He stepped closer.
"But look! She even has eyelashes."

"And fingernails," said Timothy.

Everyone crowded closer.

Mimi stepped closer, too. "Of course, she does," she told them proudly. "She has toenails, too."

Rachel opened her eyes and yawned.

Timothy leaned over to Danny. "But no teeth," he whispered.

Mimi pretended not to hear.

"Look," said Heather. "Her hands are like little stars."

Beth looked at Rachel's hands. They *are* like stars, she thought. Little pink ones.

"Her eyes are so blue," said Kelly. "She has blue eyes just like Mimi."

Mimi smiled. Rachel did have blue eyes. She had pretty blue eyes just like hers.

Mr. Cohen passed a plate full of cookies. Danny looked at every kind. Then he took a peanut butter one. Kelly took one, too.

"Mmmm, good," said Kelly.

Mimi and Beth smiled. "Peanut butter cookies are good anytime," Mimi said.

Heather sighed. "You sure are lucky. I wish I had a new baby at my house."

Lucky? Beth looked at Mimi. "I guess so," she said.

Then Rachel started to cry. "Well, sort of lucky," added Mimi.

Chapter Six

Outside it was beginning to snow.

Inside, Daddy was putting up the Christmas tree. Mimi and Beth handed him the ornaments one by one.

Mama came into the living room. "Oh, the tree is beautiful!" she said. Then she frowned. "But something is missing."

Mimi and Beth looked at each other. "Missing?"

Mama nodded. "Where are the red and green Christmas trees? I don't see them anywhere."

Mimi ran to get them from her dresser drawer.

"Here," Mama said. She carefully poked a hole in the top of each tree. Then she slipped a little hook in each hole. "Now you can hang them on the tree," she said.

Mimi hung her four green trees as high as she could reach. Beth hung her four red trees right below Mimi's.

"Now the tree looks perfect!" Mama said. She gave each of them a hug.

That night Grandpa Jack came
to dinner. "Merry Christmas!" he
called. He looked like Santa Claus.
His arms were full of presents.

Mimi and Beth helped him put the presents under the tree. Mimi peeked at the names. There was one for each of them. There was even one for Willie.

"What's in mine?" Mimi asked. She gave it a squeeze.

"A giraffe," Grandpa said.

"Really!" Mimi said. "Is it really a giraffe?"

Grandpa winked at her. "You'll see on Christmas morning."

Soon everyone was busy in the kitchen. Mama was washing the lettuce. Daddy was peeling the potatoes. Mimi and Beth set the table.

Suddenly Rachel began to cry.

"What's the matter with my

little girl?" Grandpa picked Rachel
up. He jiggled her in his arms,
but Rachel only cried harder.

"Oh, now what do I do?"
Grandpa asked.

"I'll take her," Mimi said.

"No, let me hold her," said Beth.

"You can both hold her,"
Grandpa said.

Mimi and Beth squeezed into the old rocker. Grandpa put Rachel in Mimi's arms. Beth held Rachel's feet.

Mama handed Mimi the bottle. "Maybe she's hungry," she said.

Rachel didn't want the bottle. She waved her arms and fussed.

"Here," said Beth. "I know what she wants." Beth slid forward and gave the rocker a gentle push with her foot.

Creak, creak.

Mimi and Beth and Rachel rocked back and forth, back and forth. Rachel stopped fussing. Her blue eyes looked up at Mimi and Beth.

"I think she knows us," whispered Beth.

Rachel's fingers curled around Mimi's thumb. "I think she does," Mimi said softly.

Slowly, slowly Rachel's eyes began to close.

Mimi held Rachel very quietly. Beth rocked the rocker very gently. Soon Rachel was asleep.

Grandpa tiptoed into the living room. He smiled at Beth and Mimi. "Well," he whispered, "how do you like being big sisters?"

Mimi and Beth looked down at Rachel. "Fine," they whispered back. "Just fine."